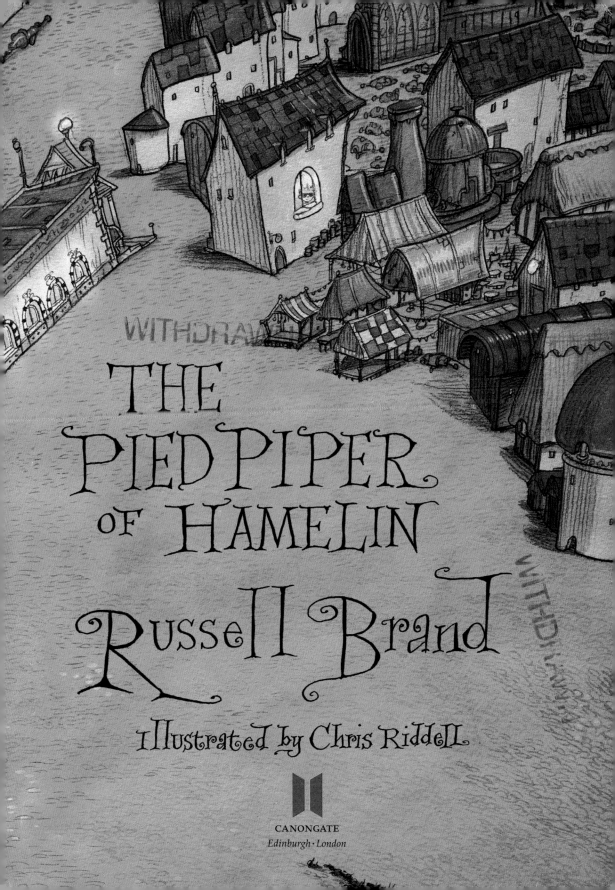

THE PIED PIPER OF HAMELIN

Russell Brand

Illustrated by Chris Riddell

CANONGATE

Edinburgh · London

NCe

upon a time, a mysterious time that exists through a window in your mind, a time that seemed, to those present, exactly like now does to us, except their teeth weren't so clean and more things were wooden, there was a town called Hamelin.

The people of Hamelin were a pompous bunch who loved themselves and their town so much that if it were possible they would have spent all day zipped up in a space suit smelling their own farts. But space suits hadn't been invented in their dimension so they couldn't.

Instead they held endless puffed-up competitions and parades to see who grew the best vegetables or had the nicest garden, or whose pig had the prettiest teats, but the most prestigious of the contests was the annual pageant for **The Most Gorgeous Child in Hamelin**.

The pageants were a good way of checking that things were nice and neat and normal. The Hamelinians liked things nice and neat and normal. They liked Hamelin the way it was: tidy and trim and controlled. They didn't like anyone or anything coming in to Hamelin and upsetting its perfect borders and lines. Not ideas, not strangers, not animals. If they needed new people, the Hamelinians thought, they'd make them themselves: Hamelinian children, perfectly fashioned in Hamelin.

Now if you ask me, the children of Hamelin were
a wretched posse of pink-cheeked snot-sacks;
guzzling chocolate and gurgling lemonade,
belching up grog with
pockets full of mulch
and bottoms
full of stink.

GROG:
a stinking brew,
or pus out of
a dark place
or a bottle.

There wasn't a kid in Hamelin I'd go near
with a 'gorgeousness' trophy unless it was to

bosh 'em over
the noggin.

Alright, okay, I'll be honest, as honesty is meant to be SO important, of all the town's children there was one I wouldn't love to slug in the guts with a wooden hammer.

His name was Sam and he had a gammy leg, that is to say it was all withered and thin like a sparrow's leg. Lame you'd call him in Hamelinian.

Sam had just turned up on planet Earth with a deficient limb, he popped out his mum and the Hamelinian doctors informed her sniffily that Sam was odd.

"I shall love him just as much or maybe more," she chirped. The doctors, unprofessionally, it should be said, rolled their eyes.

"There's a place for kids like him on the outskirts of town; for naused-up nippers with bulging eyes, with skin too yellow or blue or not pink enough, with thin legs or too much fingers. We can fling him in the cart and he'd be there by tea time," said the top doctor, checking his giant, fancy watch that could do things he never needed it to do.

Sam's Mum, even though she'd lived in Hamelin for ages and knew people could be right divs, was pretty appalled.

"No way! I love this lad! He's stopping with me. His name is Sam," she pulled Sam in all tight like a jacket potato.

"Maybe he'd be happier in a bizarre depository for unfinished kids on the outskirts of town," said Sam's Dad, who was tugging on a fag out the window, just below the 'No Smoking' sign.

DIVS: real stupid nit wits.

Sam's Dad was a man who found it hard to love people because his parents were a bit aloof and self-involved. We should be empathetic, that means try to understand and not judge him, but I feel so bad for little newborn Sam that I think I'm just going to cut the swine right out of the story.

There. We'll never see him again.

L uckily Sam had his mum and she more than made up for having one leg a bit thinner than other people's legs and even thinner than his own other leg.

"Sam, you are perfect as you are, a perfect expression of the love I feel for you. I wouldn't change any aspect of you because I wouldn't want to tinker with perfection." Which was a nice thing to say and gave Sam a lot of comfort and peace inside, which he needed because whenever he went outdoors all the other kids in Hamelin were total jerks to him.

When he was small and learning to walk he'd hobble along on crutches trying his best to join in with the turd-kicking puke-buckets of the town, but they'd always holler the vilest abuse at the lad.

"Bog off Sam, you twig-legged oddball!"

"Yeah! Go limp off into a ditch."

"You are a nobody and you'll never amount to nothing!"

Whilst this hurt Sam in his little tummy he'd never show it. He'd fib and say, "Sticks and stones may break my bones but names will never hurt me." That actually encouraged some kids, who took stuff too literally, to throw stones at him. I'll have to think of a better comeback, thought Sam, rubbing the bump on his head.

By far and away the worst of the booger-scoffing, stone-throwing Hamelin tot-rotters was Fat Bob. He was a rotund sphere of chocolate-coated self-regard. Probably because he had won the most **Gorgeous Child** pageants, not to mention a series of less important but still prestigious contests – loudest burp, for three years running, wettest fart, district finalist, and the Hamelin beige rosette for slickest poop.

This last gave him such pride that he wore it emblazoned on his chest most mornings and once, on half term, when emotions ran high for Fat Bob, he was so eager to get the thing on he'd pierced his own rubbery nipple with the pin.

He usually wore a sailor suit, like Donald Duck's one but with underpants on, he had one gold tooth, very scabby knees and his cheekaboos were so rosy and plump that if I thought I could get away with it I would prick 'em with a fork. Fat Bob, like a lot of bully-boys, ran with a gang. That way he didn't have to face up to his own feelings or the quiet sobbing in the corner of his mind, he could live in the colourful din of the day creating a racket with his crew, scorching the elegant beauty of the moment with chants and marches.

Gretchen, who was usually in his orbit, adored Fat Bob. The cheeks, the rosette, the blooming circle of blood around his right nipple, all to her seemed like the marks of a good sort.

Now, Gretchen is what you'd call gorgeous. Tall, tall like a tower in Castilla with a donkey being shoved off it (they do that, you know), dark blue eyes like the deepest oceans where people dump their rubbish (this also happens) and her hair a tangled meadow of gold that had no obvious connotations of cruelty or irresponsibility. I have to admit, she had great hair.

HAMELIN HAIR

JUNE ISSUE

CONNOTATIONS: stuff that you reckon cos of other stuff that you've seen.

Dennis hung around Fat Bob too. Dennis was so unremarkable that he pretended to be whatever was required of him in any given moment just to fit in. Look at the drawings of him – he's always different. See.

Today was a special day for the townspeople, the most important day of their year. It was finally, after 364 of the most boring days imaginable, time for **The Most Gorgeous Child in Hamelin** pageant. In Hamelin they don't have Jesus or Buddha or Mohammed so there was no Christmas, or any of that. They pretended to worship a goat called Ezra who jumped off the sun and created all the galaxies by sicking up chocolate milk and spinning it into planets. It's a daft belief system, but the Hamelinians didn't mind because they only paid attention to the bits that suited them. On Ezramus Day the townspeople sat around and told stories about why they were the kindest person in Hamelin. It's pretty lame. For them, **The Most Gorgeous Child in Hamelin** pageant is the big one, a chance to really let rip and enjoy life.

Today everyone was really feeling the vibe – there were banners, fireworks (which in the daytime are just invisible explosions), stalls selling amazing candy and lamb legs dipped in sherbet (a Hamelinian delicacy), local news crews bustling and smiling (Good Morning, Hamelin! Get Your Perfect Bottom Out Of Bed!), everyone's hair was immaculately combed and their clothes were ironed so straight that they were scared to move.

The parents that had children in the pageant, like Fat Bob's Dad, Gretchen's Mum and a bunch of others, stood around licking lollipops, sipping hot wine (a treasured tradition) and bragging about their vile brats.

"Bob is so delicious," said Fat Bob's Dad, proudly watching as his son pushed a wasp into a baby's open mouth. Fat Bob's Dad dressed as if he was twenty-five years old, which he wasn't, and as if he worked in a shop selling Italian menswear, which he didn't. He sluiced down his hot wine as if he thought it needed to get in his guts quickly before someone else nicked it. He gurgled on about his nasty son.

"He's so strong and sensitive," mused Fat Bob's Dad wistfully, as if he was talking about his boyfriend and not his son, "and his hair smells as sweet as great Ezra's breath." Only the vicar really minded that the name of Ezra, the goat that the Hamelinians had built a self-serving religion around, was being used in such a trivial context and he couldn't say anything, he had too many secrets. No one else in Hamelin cared much about using Ezra's name in vain, they only cared about things that give you a buzz or get you attention.

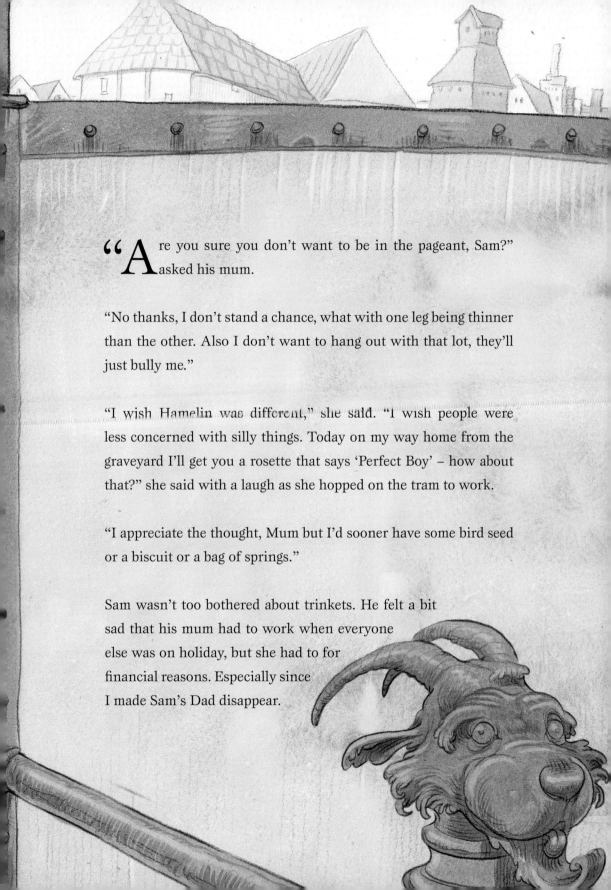

"Are you sure you don't want to be in the pageant, Sam?" asked his mum.

"No thanks, I don't stand a chance, what with one leg being thinner than the other. Also I don't want to hang out with that lot, they'll just bully me."

"I wish Hamelin was different," she said. "I wish people were less concerned with silly things. Today on my way home from the graveyard I'll get you a rosette that says 'Perfect Boy' – how about that?" she said with a laugh as she hopped on the tram to work.

"I appreciate the thought, Mum but I'd sooner have some bird seed or a biscuit or a bag of springs."

Sam wasn't too bothered about trinkets. He felt a bit sad that his mum had to work when everyone else was on holiday, but she had to for financial reasons. Especially since I made Sam's Dad disappear.

Sam's contemplation was interrupted in typical fashion when Gretchen, Fat Bob and Dennis, who, at great personal expense had re-animated some road-kill with cogs and twigs and primitive electronics. Sam looked at this ingenious new threat – a mangy rabbit, a headless badger and an inside-out fox.

The trio of adored wretches chortled as they set their **mechanical**

woodland
zombie
army after Sam.

He sighed as those who know suffering do when a new horror is unleashed, and swung with gymnastic efficiency between his crutches and headed to the hills.

It was as if some magical being who lives in the sky and the trees, the rivers and beneath our thoughts knew the people of Hamelin were no good, for on this day, their most cherished day, without warning, a gang of rats bowled into the town and began causing a right rumpus. I assure you that these were no ordinary rats. They were as big as cats and afraid of nothing. They were oily and slick and wore eye patches and carried flick-knives and could machine-gun butt-pellets out of their egg-holes whenever they fancied.

RUMPUS:
noisy trouble
like smashing
up your room
is a rumpus.

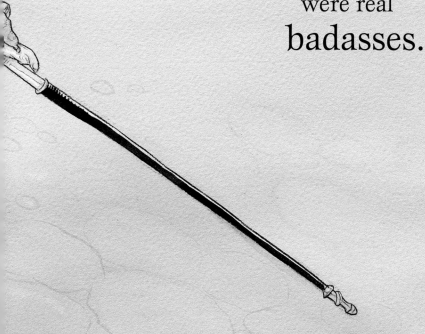

Even though they called themselves an anarcho-egalitarian rat collective (that means there's no rules and no one's in charge), in reality Casper was in charge. He had too much fur on his body and none on his head – he looked like a pink egg made of skin in a Turkish wrestler's armpit. In his constant attendance were a pair of ratty twins – Gianna and Paul – who were both his wives. In anarcho-egalitarian rat-collectives polygamy (more than one wife) is common.

It's not as common for one

of the wives to be male

but these rats

were real

badasses.

They lived mostly on land but they were like hairy little villains of the sea.

PI-RATS!

The complacent, lazy folks of Hamelin had no idea how to cope with this new menace, they were used to the easy life and didn't like trouble or confrontation. Especially not with opponents that couldn't be easily crushed. Especially not on this day, of all days, a special day, a time for fun, celebration and gorgeous children.

"What shall I do?!"

sobbed the startled butcher as a greasy rat pizzled a pint of warm, yellow belly fizz onto a pile of sherbet-covered lamb legs.

"This is unholy!"

squelched a washerwoman as a skinhead rat slashed up her pristine 'Go Gretchen' banner with his claws.

"This is twisting my melon man!" yelped Fat Bob's Dad as the twin rats daubed 'WE RULE' on Fat Bob's fat face with a spoonful of their own bum custard.

The rat gang were on a crazy trip – remember these guys have no rules – they play with matches, Casper torched a climbing frame in the school playground.

NO RULES!

A baby rat, who should've been asleep but had no rat bedtime, jazzed himself dizzy until he was sick out of his bottom all over **The Most Gorgeous Child in Hamelin** trophy!

NO RULES!

Three rat Siamese triplets joined at the hip and chanting hip-hop rhymes poured sugar into the tanks of all the wooden cars in the car park where the pageant was being held! The cars all chugged into a sweet stew of sticky nonsense. A TRAFFIC JAM!

NO RULES!

The rat twins that Casper married were actually brother and sister and none of the other rats ever even mentioned it.

Mind you, Casper was volatile. These lawless, filthy, scumbag rats were rearranging Hamelin with nothing in mind but mad rat urges.

They used their rat egg-hole-poo-gun-machine-bums to rat-a-tat-tat the pageant into a dung-covered muck-hurricane.

They used their vicious little-lellow claws to rip up all the posters.

They smashed shop windows using stones and sticks that were lying around from when Fat Bob and his gang had been bullying Sam earlier.

The Hamelinians fled squawking like crows. They hissed like cats. They whined like dogs.

One bloke done a poo by a lamppost like a tramp. To be fair it was Jeff, who had been homeless for five years since his wife left him and his army pension was cancelled. Still it added to the escalating sense of chaos.

The people scrammed in cowardly haste to what had been their perfect homes and bolted the doors and pulled down the metal shutters (one of the only metal things in Hamelin were the shutters). The place was battered and broken and mangled and the rats would not abate.

S am was high on a hill just outside of town, feeding the sparrows that lived there. He watched and wondered what it all meant.

The panicked townsfolk decided something must be done, so a committee of the Hamelinians with the loudest voices and the worst breath was formed and they went to confront the Mayor. Noreen had been mayor for a month and the job had helped her feel a lot better about herself as she'd always been the spindliest of her nine sisters. Plus she was a spinster (not yet married), and there's only so much spin a person can take. At least now she was mayor – a high-status job that made her feel better about her knees and lack of husband. But now the Mayor had a crisis on her bony hands. She smoothed her silken sash that said 'Mayor' on it in massive neon letters.

"Do something or we'll go out of business!" bawled a candlestick-maker.

"This is unacceptable," whispered a spy.

"I knew we shouldn't have a woman for a mayor," said Sexist Dave, sensing an opportunity to advance his own agenda – sexism, which is when you think boys are better than girls.

The slick, bandito rat gang even had the gall to show up at the town meeting where they were being discussed. They gnawed people's heels as they spoke, and squealed and burped over the Hamelin town song. They jived and danced on the Mayor's table as she frantically tried to maintain order. Casper plucked her thick, false eyelashes and made himself a kind of grass-skirt and did some hula dancing. **These rats were up for anything**.

Sam stayed away from the meeting. Fat Bob and his cronies had given him a real beating earlier. Gretchen had distracted him with her mesmerising beauty, while Dennis lathered his crutches in honey. Predictably some bees came wading in like a yellow and black cloud that rained stings instead of droplets and things could've got real bad had it not been for the fortunate arrival of three rats driving Sexist Dave's wooden moped (sticker on back reads 'Get behind me, ladies – it's where you belong') forcing Hamelin's most repulsive earwax-lickers to leg it.

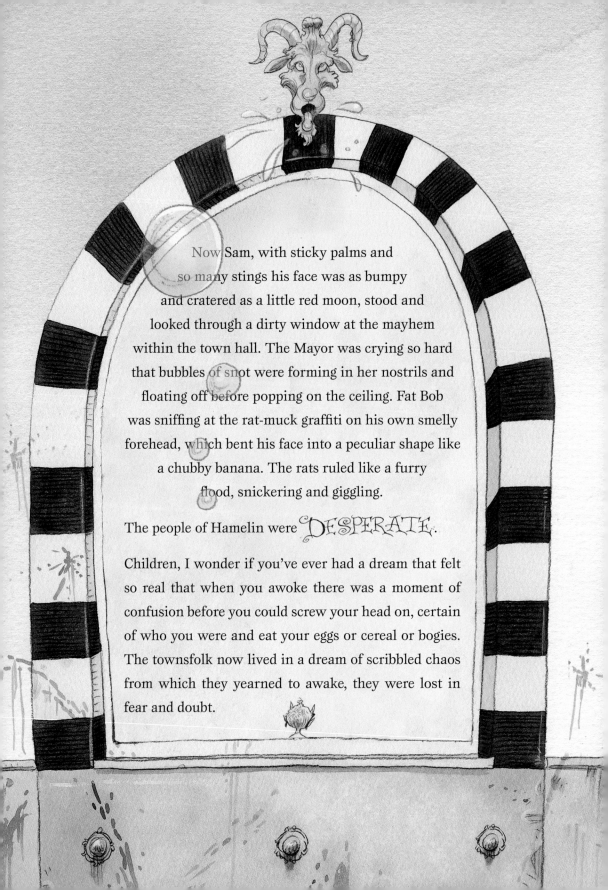

Now Sam, with sticky palms and so many stings his face was as bumpy and cratered as a little red moon, stood and looked through a dirty window at the mayhem within the town hall. The Mayor was crying so hard that bubbles of snot were forming in her nostrils and floating off before popping on the ceiling. Fat Bob was sniffing at the rat-muck graffiti on his own smelly forehead, which bent his face into a peculiar shape like a chubby banana. The rats ruled like a furry flood, snickering and giggling.

The people of Hamelin were DESPERATE.

Children, I wonder if you've ever had a dream that felt so real that when you awoke there was a moment of confusion before you could screw your head on, certain of who you were and eat your eggs or cereal or bogies. The townsfolk now lived in a dream of scribbled chaos from which they yearned to awake, they were lost in fear and doubt.

Then, sudden and exciting like a slash of glistening wee-wee on a blanket

of fresh snow, the thick rat-breath air was sliced by the sound of a pipe.

They Say Cometh the Hour Cometh the Man

That means when a situation demands it, the right person – it could be a woman, despite what Sexist Dave would tell you – will appear.

This was the hour and in this case the man was a Piper.

A Pied Piper.

This Piper had just sidled into the hall. Only Sam had noticed him. The Pied Piper didn't think much about silly things like man or woman, black or white, day or night. His Pied Piper mind lived beyond all that. Beyond opposites.

His clothes were a patchwork of black and white, and his eyes were chequered, I suppose to make this point. He was not happy and not sad. Not good or bad. He was neither ordinary nor magical. He was like nobody they'd ever seen before. The room fell silent but for his strange music. And for the first time since they arrived the rat gang looked nervous.

SIDLED:
walked quietly
and sneakily.

S am watched this man with quiet regard. Sam was more awake than the other kids because he spent more time alone, reflecting. He knew the Piper must be special.

His music was like writing on the sky that drew the eye and slowed the breath.

"Seems to me you've got yourself a rat problem," said the Piper, removing his silver pipe from his thin lips.

"What makes you say that?" said the Mayor, absent-mindedly pointing to her garish sash with a bony digit – keen to establish authority with the stranger and seem cool, even though there was a rat trembling in her bra.

"We are just addressing our rat problem now, you peculiar man," said Fat Bob's Dad. He always thought he'd be a better mayor. The Piper surveyed the melee – that means he looked at all the madness.

"I reckon this geezer's a wrong 'un," said Gretchen's Mum.

IRON YOU OUT. Wallop flat.

"I'll iron you out, you mug!" said her dad.

Gretchen's parents were well up for a scrap. It meant they didn't have to think about their relationship which was going badly.

"What if we did have a rat problem?" began the Ice Cream Man. "What would you do? Judging from your outrageous clothes you've just come from a mental hospital!"

The Piper was not a man who took kindly to hostility and the lingo of sarcasmo, so he played a few bars on his silver flute. The music rolled through the town hall connecting the minds of everyone there with invisible threads of dancing light and they knew then that the Piper could help them and their pride began to diminish, that means, get smaller.

LINGO: language.
SARCASMO: sarcastic.

OH DAD, YOUR BUM GAS SMELLS DELICIOUS!

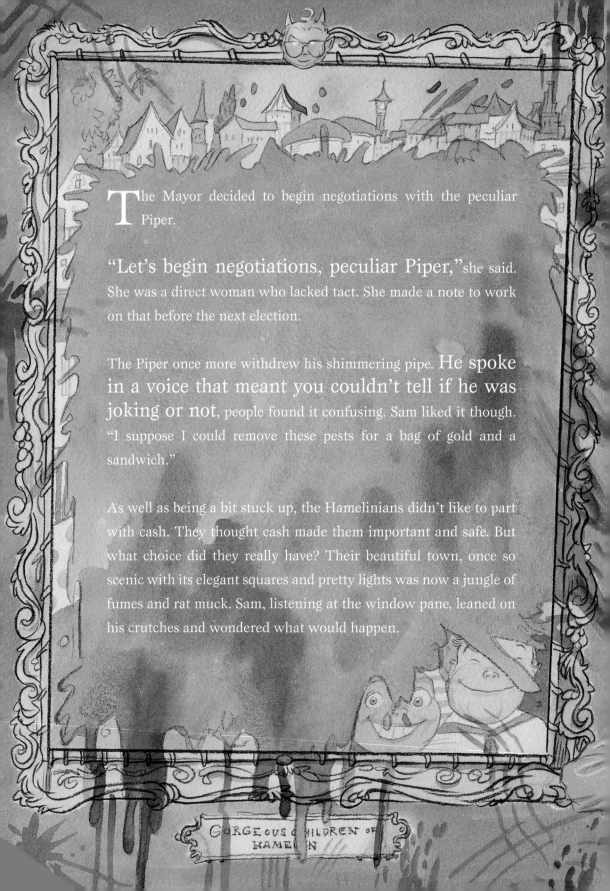

The Mayor decided to begin negotiations with the peculiar Piper.

"Let's begin negotiations, peculiar Piper," she said. She was a direct woman who lacked tact. She made a note to work on that before the next election.

The Piper once more withdrew his shimmering pipe. He spoke in a voice that meant you couldn't tell if he was joking or not, people found it confusing. Sam liked it though. "I suppose I could remove these pests for a bag of gold and a sandwich."

As well as being a bit stuck up, the Hamelinians didn't like to part with cash. They thought cash made them important and safe. But what choice did they really have? Their beautiful town, once so scenic with its elegant squares and pretty lights was now a jungle of fumes and rat muck. Sam, listening at the window pane, leaned on his crutches and wondered what would happen.

GORGEOUS CHILDREN OF HAMELIN

Fat Bob's Dad cleared his throat, which was always full of green stuff (he should've seen the doctor but was too embarrassed). He began to speak.

If he'd been typing instead of talking the font would have been called because he was a man with a plan.

"You can have your sandwich now, Piper," he offered, "as we do seem to require your assistance. But the bag of gold will not be issued until the rats have successfully been extricated." That is a posh word for got rid of.

The glint-eyed Piper didn't even seem to move. The glint-eyed Piper didn't live in the world of men and rats. The glint-eyed Piper had no need for sandwiches and gold as he lived by a higher code. His pipe was a connection to a secret thing, a secret that we all keep in our quiet minds. We hear it whisper when we are at peace, when we ain't all wrapped up in a need for candy or attention and crap.

"You are a shrewd businessman, Fat Bob's Dad," said the Piper, and the Mayor felt a little jealous.

"What day would you like the rats gone?"

"At once!" carped the Mayor, thrusting a ham sandwich that she fortunately had in her mayor's bag in the Piper's direction. He looked at it down his slender beak.

"I'm vegetarian," he said.

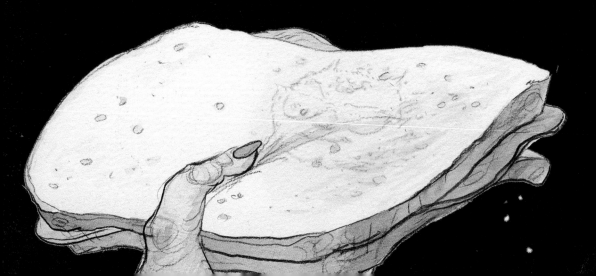

It was agreed that when the town's proud clock struck six o'clock, the Piper would remove the rats, and there was a lot of hubbub about how he'd do it.

"I reckon he'll smash their skulls with his pointy boots," said Gretchen, pulling a string of bubble gum all long from her gob in a way that got her a lot of attention.

"Perhaps he'll eat them," said Fat Bob.

"Nonsense," began his dad. "He'll dig a hole as big as a hippo and shove those damn rats down it."

The rats themselves tried to carry on as normal, kicking up a fuss and smashing vases and heirlooms but their confidence had definitely been dented. Casper, who when under pressure had a tendency to show off, set fire to a child's pram in the town square and Flamenco danced all round it. But even as he clicked and snapped and whirled, secretly checking there was no baby in the pram, he was nervous inside. Everybody wondered what would happen: the Mayor, the kids, the rats.

What do you think will happen, children? Look around inside your mind, listen to what it says . . .

Feel What it is telling you?

The Piper strolled down
from the tallest hill
in Hamelin where he'd
been sitting perfectly
still whilst watching the
clouds. Occasionally he'd
blow gentle notes from
his pipe and they'd travel
effortlessly through the air
like tiny vibrating birds and
mingle with the clouds.

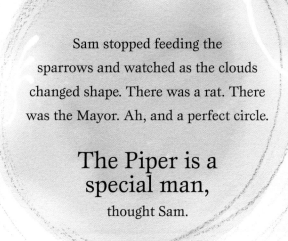

Sam stopped feeding the
sparrows and watched as the clouds
changed shape. There was a rat. There
was the Mayor. Ah, and a perfect circle.

The Piper is a
special man,

thought Sam.

Everyone gathered around the clock in the square, as it was 5.59 p.m. Then, as the clock struck six, the Piper mooched into view, his pipe swinging at his hip from a leather holster. It was really cool. The sun was going down and the sky was filled with crazy shaped clouds that only Sam noticed.

"Come along, Piper," said Fat Bob's Dad. "It's six o'clock. You've had your sandwich. It's time to get rid of these rat bags."

"Yes," added the Mayor, adjusting her hair. She knew that Fat Bob's Dad was really taking the lead in this issue and decided to act a bit tough. "We the people of Hamelin will happily give you your gold just as soon as the plague is ameliorated." This is a word so fancy it lives in its own mansion, but it just means made better.

The clock made its sixth chime. "Now it's six!" said the glint-eyed Piper. A rat that was eating his discarded ham sandwich looked up fearfully. All the rats paused. The Piper silently drew in a long breath through his long nose.

The glint-eyed Piper knew that each breath we take is borrowed.

The glint-eyed Piper knew that all things are connected – the clouds, the people, the rats, the pipe, the music.

All things are connected by invisible threads.

The people of the town didn't know that, they only cared about things they can see and eat and get prizes for. "Hurry up," shouted Fat Bob's Dad even though it wasn't even one second since the sixth chime. He didn't like to be patient.

The Pied Piper's eyes rolled back in his head so all you could see were the whites. His lips wrapped around the pipe. The borrowed breath rushed from his black and white lungs and filled the fuselage of the silver flute. His nimble fingers danced along the holes in the shaft like limbless ballerinas.

FUSELAGE:
main bit of an
aeroplane or tube.

And if the people of the town had been looking properly they'd have seen that the Piper, the pipe, the beautiful music that was even now pouring across the square like golden wine, and the sky were all blurred, that the lines between them were imaginary.

Only Sam could see this.

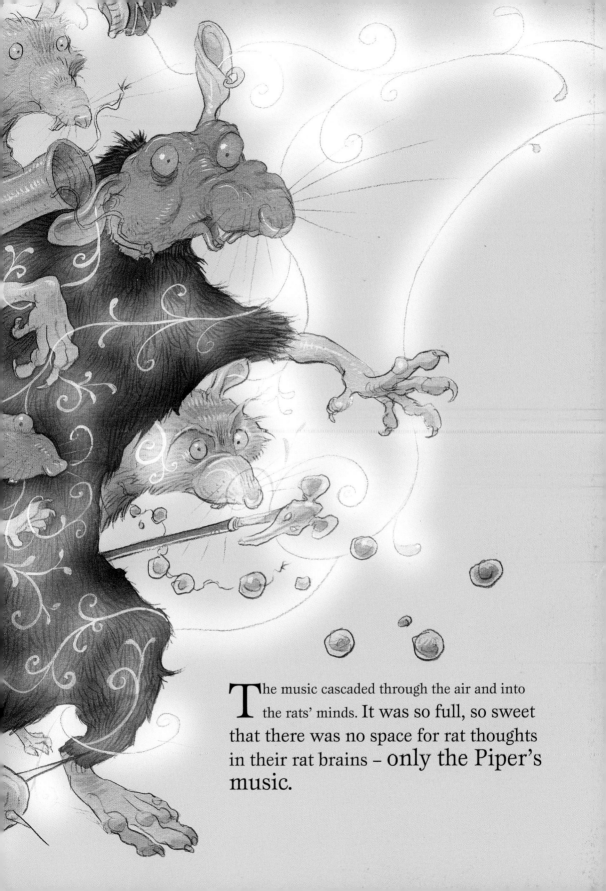

The music cascaded through the air and into the rats' minds. It was so full, so sweet that there was no space for rat thoughts in their rat brains – only the Piper's music.

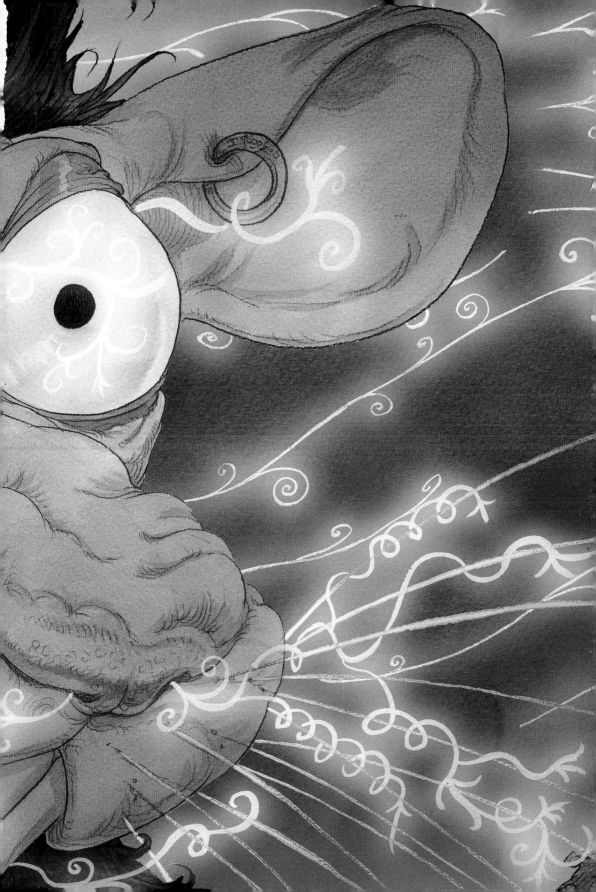

He

The tiny tunnels in the rats' brains
tangled with the music and the
music led to the pipe and the pipe led to the Piper
and the Piper began to dance a gently demented jig.

And he danced out of the square and he danced into the hills
and he danced to the sound of his own pipe and the rats
became as one like a river of shimmering fur.
They swirled about his spiky feet.

a river of

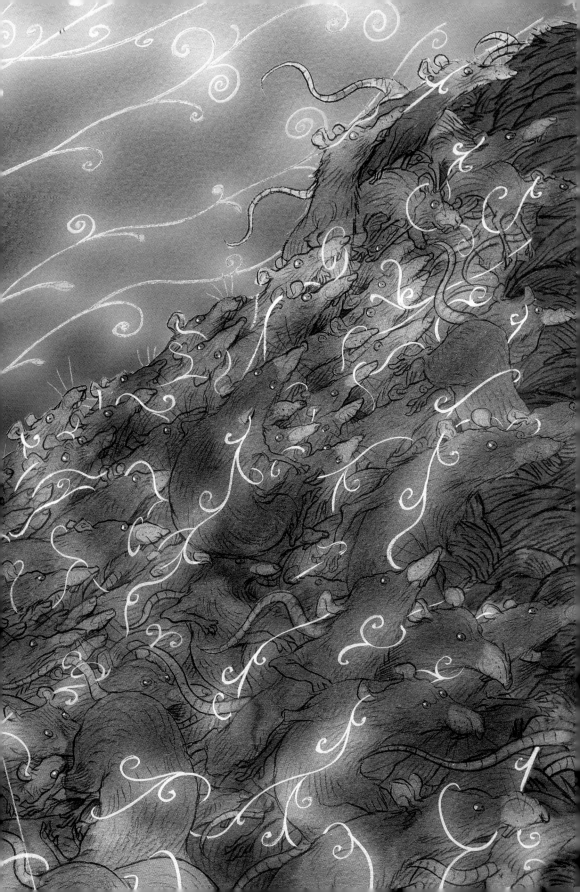

Like a jagged star on the horizon the Piper stood, the rats all about him. A quiet hurricane whirred about his legs. The square and the town was pristine, neat as if the rats and the Piper had never been there at all. Only Sam saw that the clock still chimed six. Only Sam saw that time hadn't moved at all.

The rats and the Piper had all gone from view.

The music could no longer be heard.

There was a silence, children, a silent relief.

And if the people of Hamelin had been smarter they would have been grateful in their rejoicing. But as they laughed and patted each other on the back, it was kind of like they forgot about the Piper. Everybody whooped and sang:

"The rats are gone!
The rats are gone!
The rats are gone!
What a fantastic day!"

"How clever of me to employ the Piper," blurted the Mayor.

"I think it was my idea," said Fat Bob's Dad.

"The rats probably would have left anyway," said Sexist Dave, even though the issue did not involve gender discrimination.

"Hamelin is a fine place!" sang the children and everyone was buzzing. It was a really good vibe, baby! The Mayor announced that **The Most Gorgeous Child in Hamelin** Pageant would be staged at once and the crowd roared with spineless appreciation. Sexist Dave suggested dancing girls in skimpy outfits and everyone said that was fine.

Fat Bob and the other favourites rushed home to scrub up. Homeless Jeff was politely ushered out of the square, his vagrancy always an obstacle to unbridled shallow beauty. Fat Bob won the pageant of course and strutted like a portly peacock with the hastily rinsed trophy wedged in the folds of his clammy belly. The town song was put on, a feast was organised, cakes were baked and sherbet lamb-legs scoffed. Everyone put on their best stuff and nobody considered the departed Piper.

S am thought this was a pretty sordid
state of affairs so he sat on his own
by the fountain and reflected on the Piper
and the clouds.

WE BEAT THE RATS
FEAST

"Go to the feast though, Sam – you'll have a nice time." Sam's Mum was so busy polishing graves all day that she didn't understand the complex troubles of Sam's social arrangements. Sam didn't mind.

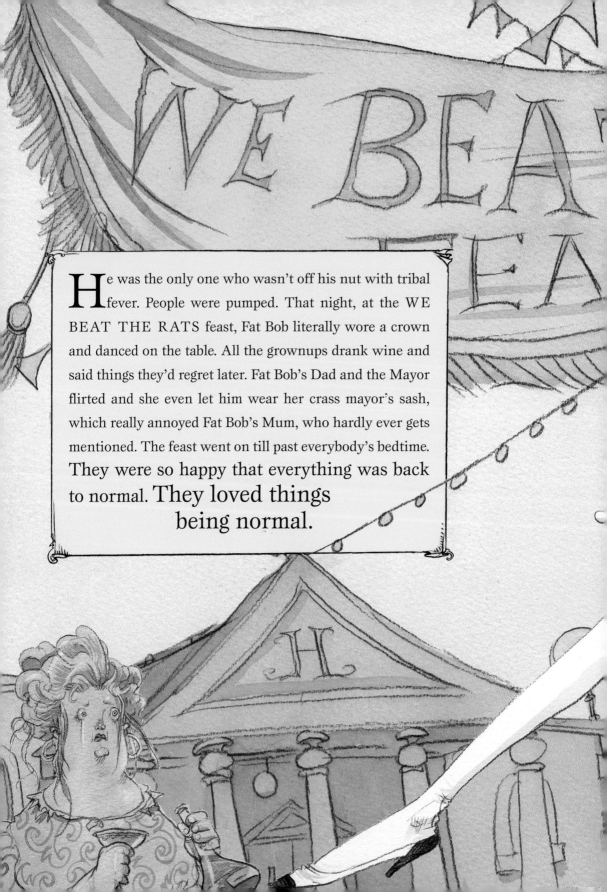

He was the only one who wasn't off his nut with tribal fever. People were pumped. That night, at the WE BEAT THE RATS feast, Fat Bob literally wore a crown and danced on the table. All the grownups drank wine and said things they'd regret later. Fat Bob's Dad and the Mayor flirted and she even let him wear her crass mayor's sash, which really annoyed Fat Bob's Mum, who hardly ever gets mentioned. The feast went on till past everybody's bedtime. They were so happy that everything was back to normal. They loved things being normal.

The next day early in the morning as the drowsy townspeople stirred to life they found the Piper already there in the middle of the square, cool as a cucumber in his pied outfit, leaning against a fountain twirling his pipe between his fingers.

Everyone felt a bit confused and threatened by the tranquil Piper so they just sort of pretended he wasn't there. The Mayor hurried past, straightening her stained sash, trying not to make eye contact. Fat Bob's Dad pretended to tie his shoelaces even though he was wearing slip-ons. The Piper played one sharp note on his pipe and if Hamelin was a window this was a stone right through it. The Pied Piper said nothing. The Pied Piper knew what was coming. The Pied Piper knew that only the moment you live in is real and everything else is pretend.

The Pied Piper put out his hand. It was awkward. Fat Bob's Dad knew, the Mayor knew, everybody knew it was . . .

Time to Pay
The Piper

What do you think the people of Hamelin did, children? My oiks, my twerps, my silly little nits. He'd played, did they pay? The music had been heard, but did they keep their word?

"I suppose you want your bag of gold," said Fat Bob's Dad, feeling confident as everyone gathered round. Sometimes grownups are bullies too.

The children stood in the crowd an' all. The adults crossed their arms. No one liked the Piper much in spite of what he'd done for them. Only Sam liked the Piper. He liked that the Piper saw through silly things like threats, rats, cruel words, thin legs, bags of gold and sandwiches. Sam stood alone, leaning against his crutches. The Piper nodded. Sam felt sure the Piper smiled at him but the Piper doesn't smile.

"Well," blurted the Mayor. "The thing is, we don't have it. Money's tight. There is a double-dip recession on." Sometimes if you say a confusing thing about money, people will back off. Others joined in.

"A bag of gold seems like a lot . . ."

"Yeah! All you did was play a dumb song."

Everyone had something to say but no one was being very honest. "The way we feel," said Fat Bob's Dad, "is that the rat problem was never that bad."

"They probably would have left anyway. It was getting cold and rats hate cold," said a scientist.

"Yes, it's likely a coincidence that the rats left. We can't pay you for a coincidence, it doesn't make economic sense," offered the bank manager. The people were beginning to enjoy telling these crazy lies. Sexist Dave, who was still a bit drunk from the night before, actually claimed that he liked rats.

The glint-eyed Piper looked on. The glint-eyed Piper had no time for lies. The glint-eyed Piper dealt only in truth.

The townspeople – the grownups and the children – closed in on the Piper. There was an air of aggro, like the Piper was in trouble. Sam's grip on his crutches tightened.

"You got nerve coming to Hamelin in your crazy clothes, with your crazy nose and your crazy mad music, demanding crazy bucks for pest control," said Fat Bob's Dad.

"Yeah!" shouted the crowd, for they'd reached the point where they all felt the same.

They were a horde, a mob with one mad mind.

"You're a gangster!" screamed a policeman.

"Yeah, you're committing daylight robbery!"

Slogans were shouted. The Piper was surrounded. People's teeth grew sharper and their skin looked a little like fur.

"Get out of Hamelin!" screamed the Mayor.

"Yeah!" yawped the mob.

In spite of all this racket and rhubarb the Piper remained very calm and still. The mob roared and buckled and swayed. The children and the grownups all chanted . . .

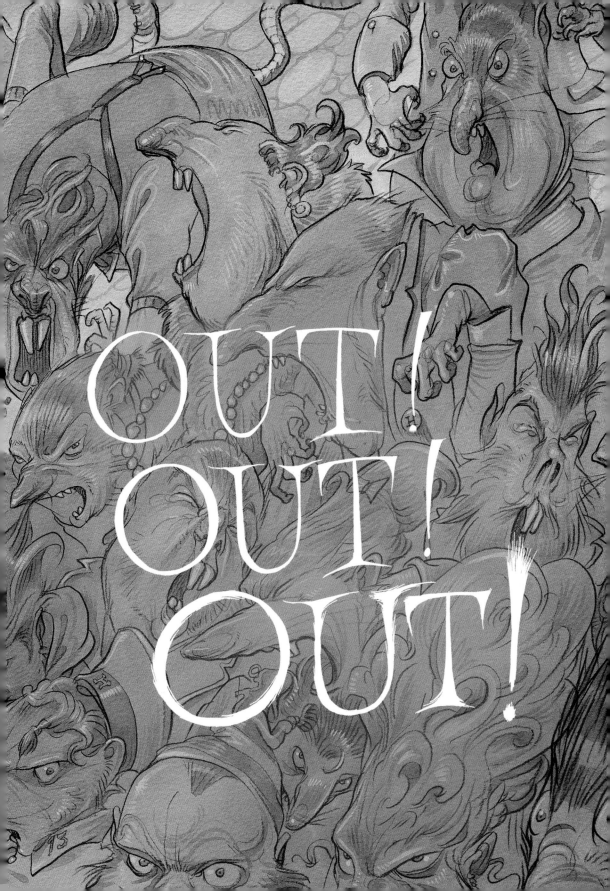

The Piper raised the pipe to his lips and played a perfect note that sliced through time like a scalpel. Then he gave them one last chance, even though he knew they wouldn't take it. They stood bristling and twitching around him. The Piper's back was against the fountain, and in the moment of stillness the Piper spoke.

"Are you sure you want me to leave?"

"Did you imagine we were joking?" bawled the Mayor. She was really in her groove now and thought this was the kind of leadership that would definitely get her re-elected.

EDGY:
low level
fear or
negativity.

"Yeah! We ain't joking," said the mob. Then someone swore and someone else kicked a lamppost – it was starting to get edgy. The Piper did not frown or smile. He didn't laugh or cry. He didn't feel happy or sad. He just raised his pipe to his lips.

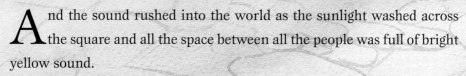

And the sound rushed into the world as the sunlight washed across the square and all the space between all the people was full of bright yellow sound.

And as the people stood there silent it was like their ears breathed this golden sound.

And all the tunnels in their minds tangled and mingled with the music like the rats' minds had.

The grownups stood still and stared.

The children swayed as the yellow sound swept around them like a strong sweet wind.

The proud clock stopped. The Piper's fingers danced. His spiky feet moved through the square and the Piper, the pipe, the music and the children moved through the square and through the narrow streets and up the tallest hill. Staring adult eyes unblinkingly teared as they realised with one mind what they had done.

The dream of Hamelin ended, as they watched the Piper like a jagged star on the horizon followed by the dancing children, and as they watched the proud clock motionless like a dead man's face, they watched the Piper and the

children

disappear

from

view.

Some people think Sam was the only child left in Hamelin because of his gammy leg all withered like a sparrow's. But you and I know that it is because he was the only person of all the children, of all the grownups, of all the people in Hamelin who didn't judge the Piper, who understood the Piper. Who understood that the most important things aren't contests and sherbet-covered lamb legs or what other people say or think about you. No, what matters are invisible things like truth, love and honour.

Some of you will wonder what happened to the children, others will wonder what happened to the Piper. Some of you may even wonder what happened to the rats.

Well this story, my darlings, my nose-pickers, my nincompoops, ain't about that – what became of them is an irrelevant secret and none of us know, but if you want to know it, you can decide yourself, in your own little brainbox.

What I can tell you is that if you go to Hamelin now, you'll find a very peaceful town, pretty but not fussy. They don't need constant contests to remind them that they're cool, the people remind each other all day long just by being nice. Strangers are always welcome and people of all shapes and colours are accepted and loved. They closed the depository for imperfect children on the outskirts of town when they realised that all children are perfect. There are a few rats there to this day but they're pretty well-behaved, the kids are all nice to one another and don't really care about who wins prizes because **the important prizes can't be won by individuals, only by us all.** You may wonder how Hamelin came to change so much from the silly, greedy, pompous town it was in our tale. Well I've told you all I know but if you want to know more, and **you should always want to know more,** you'll have to go there yourself on a bus that's in your mind. When you're there you can ask their new mayor. You'll know him when you see him, you can feel he's kind of special even though you won't know why. He's gentle and cool, he never wears the sash when he walks through the town and you'll hardly notice him limping.

TRICKSTER GLOSSARY: tricky words explained.

AGGRO: bother.

ALOOF: pompous people are aloof. They think they're better than us.

APPALLED: shocked.

BANDITO: Mexican thief. Quite cool.

BELCHING: a dirty gas out of your belly.

COMPLACENT: lazy self-regard.

CRASS: cheeky, like a fart.

CRONIES: daft mates.

DEFICIENT: broken, rubbish, not good enough. "Dad, your nappy is deficient, there's grog on your leg."

DELICACY: posh thing to eat, usually disgusting.

DEPOSITORY: place stuff gets left.

DISCRIMINATION: deciding something is not good enough or different.

EMBLAZONED: stuck on, in a fancy way.

ESCALATING: going higher, like an escalator.

GALL: nerve, cheek, front.

GARISH: bright and colourful. Might give you a headache.

GEEZER: bloke.

HEIRLOOM: old thing that you want.

HORDE: angry posse.

IMMACULATELY: without any flaws or nause ups.

MESMERIZING: hard to look away from. Makes yer mind mushy.

MULCH: crunched up, mush in yer pockets, or the bottom of your mum's bag.

NAUSED: ruined. "Mum, you've naused up that pie, it's filled with mulch."

NOGGIN: your head or nut.

PECULIAR: odd, unlike anything else.

POMPOUS: thinking you are top notch and that your blow-offs smell like flowers.

POSSE: gang, mob, group.

PRESTIGIOUS: something cool that makes you feel amazing, like a gold star or a loom band made of diamonds.

PRIMITIVE: old, basic and simple. Or like a monkey.

REANIMATED: put something back together so it can move.

ROAD-KILL: dead squished animal found on the road.

ROTUND: round and plump.

Published in Great Britain in 2014 by Canongate Books Ltd, 14 High Street, Edinburgh EH1 1TE
Copyright © Russell Brand, 2014 Illustrations © Chris Riddell, 2014 Design: Rafaela Romaya
The moral rights of the author and illustrator have been asserted
Reprographics: syntax21.co.uk
ISBN 978 1 78211 456 7
Printed and bound in Italy by Lego S.p.A